The Dance
of the Eagle and the Fish

Story by Aziz Nesin
Illustrated by Kaḡan Güner

Adapted in English for children by Alison Boyle
Translated from the Turkish by Ruth Christie

The Dance of the Eagle and the Fish

Milet Publishing Ltd
6 North End Parade
London W14 0SJ
England
Email orders@milet.com
Website www.milet.com

First published by Milet Publishing Ltd in 2001
© Milet Publishing Ltd

ISBN 1 84059 316 4

Printed and bound in Singapore by Imago

Milet

The Dance
of the Eagle and the Fish

Story by Aziz Nesin
Illustrated by Kağan Güner

Adapted in English for children by Alison Boyle
Translated from the Turkish by Ruth Christie

The ancient eagle opened his massive wings and soared.

'All around me,' thought Kartal, 'I see great skies . . . and below me I see great lands. That is all there is.'

Kartal settled on the highest rock of the highest peak. 'My eagle's-eye view of the whole earth is my power,' he declared. 'And I hold power over all.'

Kartal looked down upon his magnificent kingdom.
'I am the symbol of courage and strength, my picture is
on flags and shields,' he said. 'I appear on the crests
of thrones and the doors of palaces, and yet . . . '

Thoughts of unknown lands that he was now too old to
explore began to haunt Kartal. 'I am king of all I see,'
he cried, his grand words swept away by the icy air.

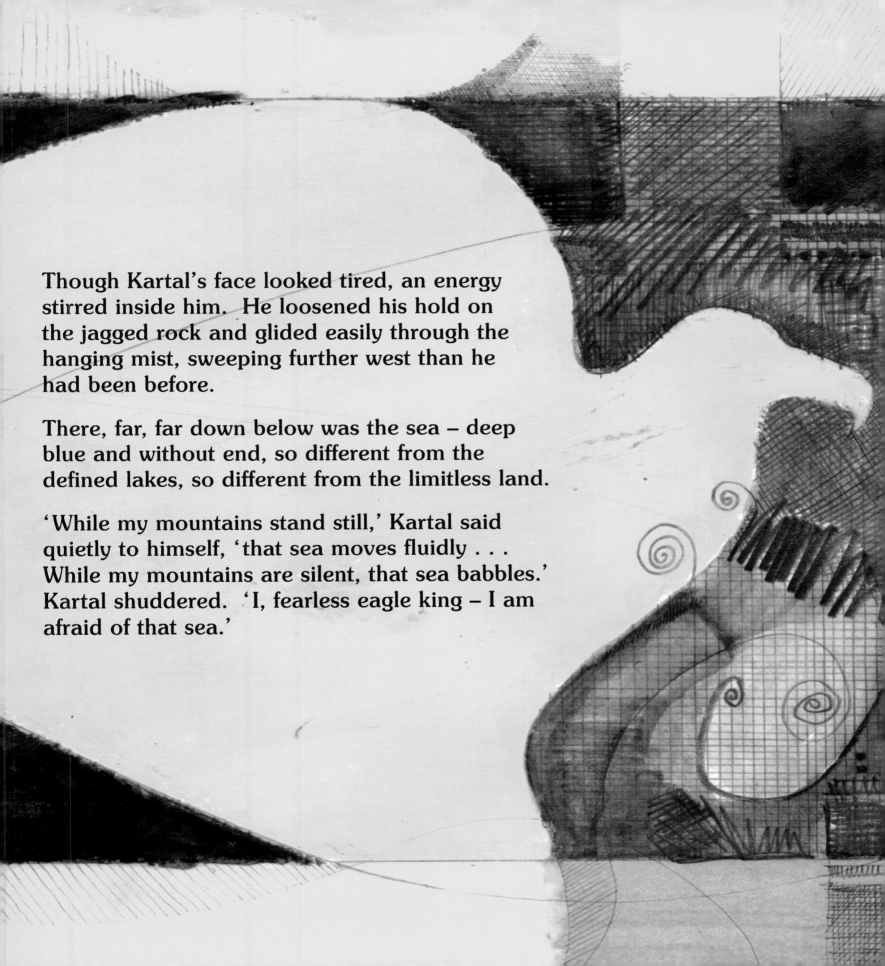

Though Kartal's face looked tired, an energy
stirred inside him. He loosened his hold on
the jagged rock and glided easily through the
hanging mist, sweeping further west than he
had been before.

There, far, far down below was the sea – deep
blue and without end, so different from the
defined lakes, so different from the limitless land.

'While my mountains stand still,' Kartal said
quietly to himself, 'that sea moves fluidly . . .
While my mountains are silent, that sea babbles.'
Kartal shuddered. 'I, fearless eagle king – I am
afraid of that sea.'

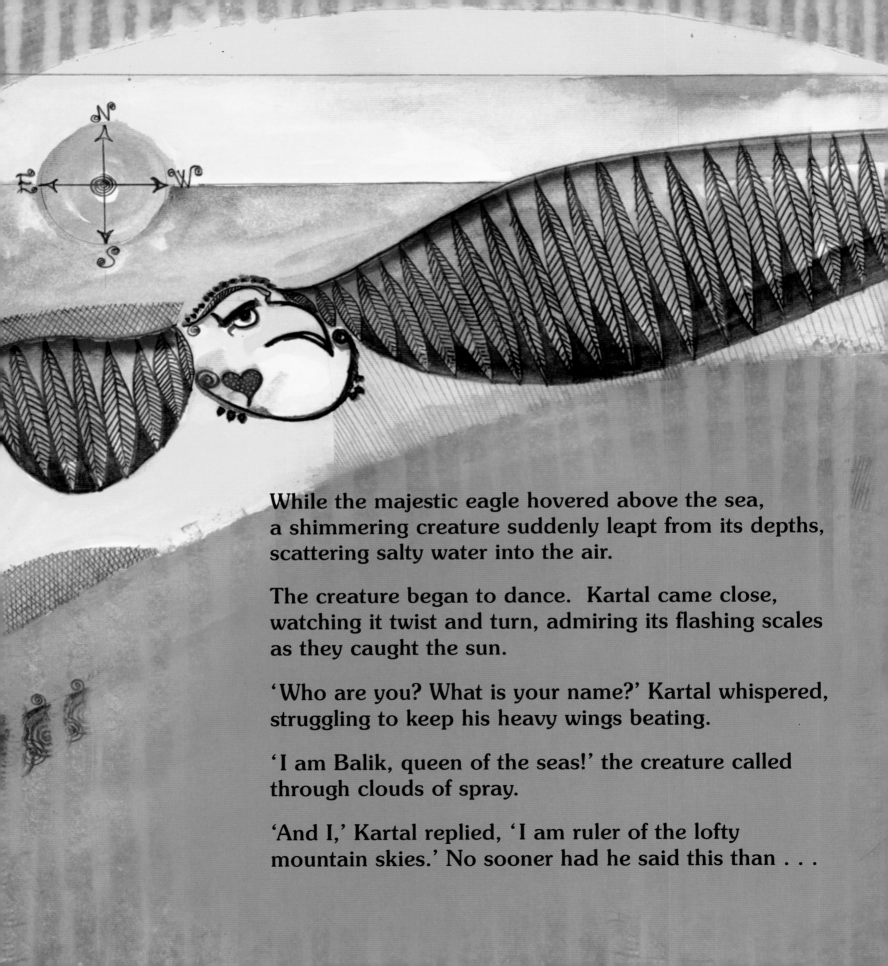

While the majestic eagle hovered above the sea,
a shimmering creature suddenly leapt from its depths,
scattering salty water into the air.

The creature began to dance. Kartal came close,
watching it twist and turn, admiring its flashing scales
as they caught the sun.

'Who are you? What is your name?' Kartal whispered,
struggling to keep his heavy wings beating.

'I am Balik, queen of the seas!' the creature called
through clouds of spray.

'And I,' Kartal replied, 'I am ruler of the lofty
mountain skies.' No sooner had he said this than . . .

. . . she was gone, into the comfort of the dark water, where she could spread her fine fins as she liked, and trail her skirt in a gauzy dance, flurrying the sand on the bed of the sea.

'All around me is my kingdom, and I am free!' sang Balik. 'Up there, in the heights of the sky, is a strange new creature who . . . who frightens me.'

Balik wove through the water thinking only of the sky creature's dance, and how she had danced with him for a short time, before falling back into the sea to breathe again.

Above the water, the old king of the skies quick-tilted his wings and swept up, up, towards his kingdom. On the way, Kartal's still-sharp eagle eye spotted a scarpering hare. Kartal dived steeply, stabbed it with the hook of his beak and curved his claws into it in an instant. He flew to a rock and killed it. Kartal ate hungrily, gasping for breath.

Until today he had been waiting for death. But now, that creature of the sea haunted his thoughts, and brought him to dream through the long, quiet night.

The young queen of the seas was troubled too. She felt more annoyed than usual with the silly wrasse racing for shelter when she came by. And she was angry with the solemn swordfish who passed her without a word.

'I am tired of them all!' snapped Balik, sweeping through the water.
'Every day, it's the same old dance. Boring, lazy creatures!'

Balik swam on, hardly noticing
the dreaded scorpion fish who
came dangerously close. Instead,
she thought all the while of the king
of the skies, who brought her to
dream through the long, fluid night.

Next morning, the king of the skies rampaged down the mountainside like an avalanche.

'I must reach the sea before my heart stops,' Kartal called, his great wings spanning wider than ever before.

At that same moment, the queen of the seas was racing to reach the exact spot where they had met. Balik leapt through the skin of the water and pierced the centre of the careful circle Kartal was drawing in the wide sky.

The two entranced creatures danced, one above, one below, until darkness came and they returned to their homes in the sky and in the sea.

When they awoke, Kartal and Balik had only one thought: that they must be together.

'Beautiful Balik,' called Kartal lovingly, showering the seas where she danced with the loveliest of mountain flowers. 'Come and live with me. I need you.'

'Beautiful Kartal,' Balik called back, showering the air where he danced with the loveliest of sea flowers, 'Live here with me. This is where I belong.'

The eagle and the fish wanted so much to be together. But something was stopping them.

At last the day came when Balik had no choice but to leave for warmer waters with the rest of the fish. But the eagle begged her to stay.

'If I stay, I'll die,' she sobbed. 'But I am willing to do this if it means we will be together.'

'NO!' Kartal exclaimed, his kingly voice shattering the waves into a thousand pieces. 'You must not die. You are young. It is I who must come with you.'

So he did, and they journeyed far, one through sea and the other through air, across many lands, until the old eagle was quite worn out.

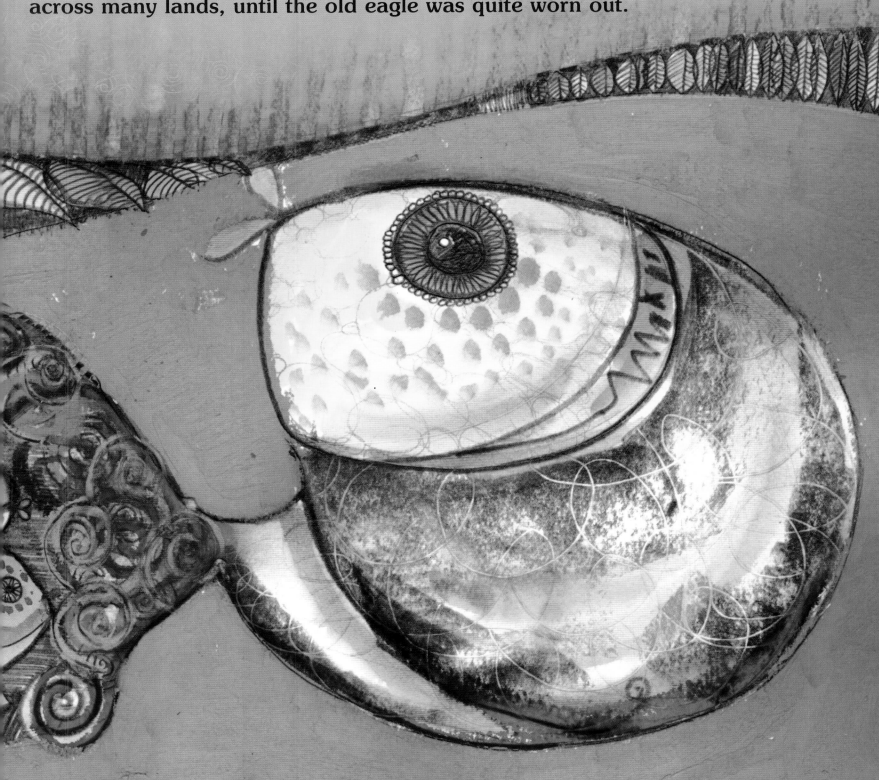

. . . until death found him in the promised place and time, and he spiralled, as was meant to be, down to that meeting place of sea and sky.

Clouds gathered, the air darkened, and Kartal was by Balik's side at last.

From the exact spot where he fell, the fish Balik rose up like a mighty eagle, powered by Kartal's great wings of love, and she danced the most beautiful dance the earth, the seas, and the skies, had ever known.